The Great Pebble Puzzle

Written by Ali Sparkes

Illustrated by Chelen Ecija

Collins

1 Written on stone

It started when Dev fell off his bike.

He was riding too fast down Puggle Lane, skidded on the bend and ended up sprawling in a clump of weeds.

He lay there, blinking. Above him floated a cloud of dandelion seeds, knocked off their stems by his sudden arrival. He could smell grass and damp earth, and the strawberry whiff of a dropped milkshake carton lying nearby. He could hear the back wheel of his bike gently clicking.

As Dev turned his head, he saw something shiny. He sat up, peering at it. It was a pebble. On one side was a tiny painting of a grey squirrel – and on the other was the word: "HELP!"

Dev stood up, rubbed his grazed knee, and looked around. Nobody was there. In the trees, he thought he saw movement ... but it was probably just a bird.

He put the pebble in his pocket and picked up the bike. Slightly shakily, he got back on and headed for home.

The last thing he expected, after putting his bike in the shed, was to find another pebble on the doorstep. This one had a painting of a white bird with a long beak and even longer legs – maybe a heron. On the back, again, he read: "HELP!"

He walked back to the lane. "Hellooo? Pebble Painter? Who are you? What do you want?" he called.

Nobody answered.

Indoors, Dev found his twin sister Alina watching TV. "Is it *you*?" he said.

Alina stared at him. "Well, I *think* it's me!" she said, standing up and frowning at herself in the mirror. "And if it's not, it's probably a killer alien who *looks* like me, so watch out!"

Dev rolled his eyes. "I meant is it you who's been painting pebbles?"

Alina took both the pebbles, turning them over. "They're lovely," she said. She was right. The little paintings were beautiful; varnished and gleaming against the plain grey stone.

"Why have they painted 'HELP!' on the back?" she asked.

Dev shrugged. He took the pebbles to his room and forgot about them ...

... until the next day, when the third pebble dropped out of the sky.

2 Rock shock

They were walking to the corner shop when Alina suddenly squeaked: "OUCH!" and she looked down to see a large pebble right where her big toe had tried to go! They looked around but couldn't see anyone hiding in the bushes.

Alina scooped it up. One side had a very small "HELP!"
painted on it. On the other side was a tiny lizard with
green and gold scales. Its tail was curved around to
its head and its eyes were round, black and shining.
It glittered like a jewel.

"Maybe a magpie found it and dropped it," said Dev.

"I'm keeping this one," said Alina, beaming and shaking her toe. "It's the best one yet!"

"But how are we meant to help?" asked Dev. "What does the Pebble Painter want us to *do*?"

In the shop, they were buying ice lollies when Dev noticed something on the till. "Hey!" he said to Mr Dillow, the shopkeeper. "Is that a painted pebble?"

Mr Dillow picked it up, smiling. "Yes – Lily found it on the doorstep first thing this morning." He called back into the house behind the shop. "Lily! Come and show Dev and Alina your stone."

His daughter came out and proudly cupped the pebble in her hands. On it was a glittering silver fish.

"Does it say 'HELP!' on the back?" asked Alina.

"It *does*," said Lily, looking surprised.

Alina held up her lizard pebble and flipped it over to the "HELP!"

"What's all that about then?" puzzled Mr Dillow. "Did *you* paint these?"

They shook their heads. "I *wish*," said Alina. "I'd love to be that good at art."

"It's a mystery," murmured Lily.

"Why don't they just *ask* for help?" said Dev, outside the shop. "I mean ... what's the point if we don't *know* what they want us to do? We're not mind readers!"

"The animals ..." said Alina. "They're clues. We need to work out what a squirrel, a heron, a lizard and a fish all have in common."

"It's just someone messing around," said Dev, peeling the plastic off his lolly and dropping it on top of the overflowing bin outside the shop. A gust of wind picked it up and blew it into the trees across the road.

CORNER SHOP

yes!
we are
open!

14

"But they must take *hours* to paint," said Alina. "That's not just messing around."

Dev shrugged. "Well, that's probably the last of them." He glanced across to the trees and thought for a moment he saw someone moving in there.

But it was probably just the ice lolly wrapper.

3 Boulder-sized clue

Dev went to Ben's house after tea. They got muddy in the garden and had to take their trainers off before they went inside for computer games.

When they came back out, Dev pulled his trainers back on. "Yeow!" He pulled one off – and another pebble fell out.

"What's that?" asked Ben.

"A painted pebble," said Dev, feeling his skin prickle. This was getting spooky. This pebble was painted with a mouse, sitting up, its tail wrapped around its tiny feet and its delicate whiskers shimmering.

"Wow!" said Ben. "Nice!"

"It's not just nice," said Dev, turning it over. "It's a message."

"Who from?" asked Ben.

"I don't know, but this is the third pebble today. I've got two more at home from yesterday and another dropped on Alina today. Lily in the corner shop found one this morning too. They've all got animals on one side and 'HELP!' on the other."

"*Weird,*" said Ben. He picked up one of his own trainers and gave a shout of surprise as something tumbled out of it. "Look! Me too!" He held out the smooth, oval stone. His animal was a moth with brown and red wings and curly antennae. And – yes – there was the "HELP!" on the back.

Ben asked indoors but
nobody had seen anyone
in the garden.

"It's a total mystery!" he said.

"But nothing mysterious
happens in Puggle!"
said Dev.

"Maybe it's a warning,"
whispered Ben.

"What ... a little painting on a pebble?!" scoffed Dev.

"This is how it STARTS," said Ben, who watched a lot of scary TV. "Then it's a rock with a wolf on it, smashing through your bedroom window ... then it's a massive boulder rolling down the road after you! With an elephant painted on it ..."

4 Mystery map

"Dev! Wake up!"

Dev groaned and sat up in bed as Alina stood over him.

"The Pebble Painter's been again!" she said. "But this one's *different*!"

She shoved another pebble in his face. "I just found it on my bedroom windowsill!"

It was large, round and flat. One side had a painting of ... Dev squinted. "Is that a *map*?"

"Yes!" said Alina. "I think it's a map of the river in Puggle Valley ... look ..." She pulled a magnifying glass out of her pyjama pocket and held it over the pebble. At once, Dev could see a blue river winding through trees and under a bridge. A sparrow hawk roosted on its railing.

"I know this place," he said.

"Yes! So do I!" said Alina. "We have to go there so we can solve the Pebble Puzzle!"

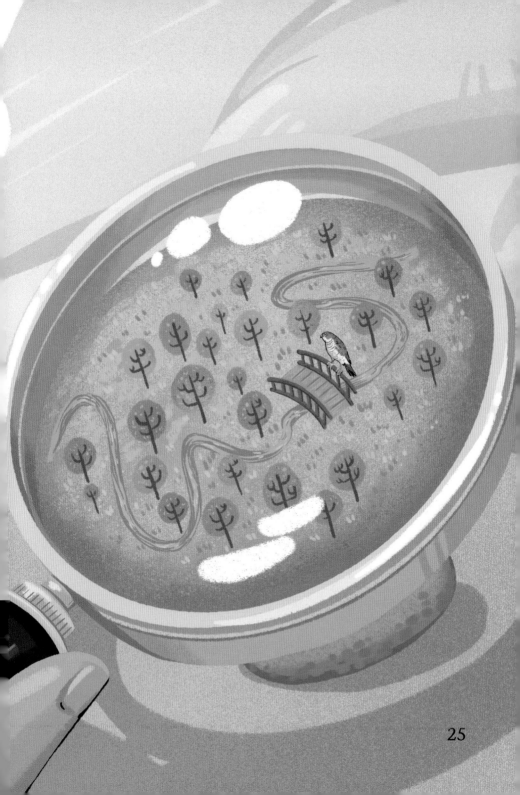

"OK ... when?"

Alina turned the pebble over. On the back, instead of "HELP!" it said: "11:30 a.m."

"What if it's a trap?" asked Dev, remembering Ben's warning.

"A *trap*?" echoed Alina.

Dev rubbed his face, embarrassed. "You know ... maybe ... someone wants to steal children so they're handing out pebbles to make them show up in the woods."

Alina considered this. "MUM!" she yelled. "If we go down to the woods with Lily and Ben, do you think we'll be OK?"

Mum peered around the door. "I'm sure you will be, but I'll meet you down there in ten minutes just in case. You must stay together, OK?"

After breakfast, they raced down to the corner shop.
Lily, helping her dad behind the counter, was surprised
to see them. "What are you two so excited about?"
she asked.

Alina held up the map pebble. "This was on my windowsill this morning," she said. "So ... we don't know what the Pebble Painter wants but we *do* know where to go to find out."

Lily pulled another two pebbles from her pockets.
"I found this on my scooter yesterday teatime," she said,
waving a long, thin stone with a diamond-patterned
serpent on it and flipping it to show the "HELP!" on
the back.

"And then … this morning, when I fetched
the newspapers off the step for Dad … this one."

In her other hand, she held an oval, flat stone. It had
the map and the time on it. "Do you know where this
is?" she asked.

"Yes," said Dev. "We're going there now. We'll get Ben, too. Are you coming?"

"Try stopping me!" said Lily.

"It could be dangerous," warned Dev. "We don't know who the Pebble Painter is."

"It's OK," said Lily. "I'm a black belt in karate."

When they got to Ben's, they found him sitting on his doorstep with three pebbles: the moth pebble he'd found yesterday, a new one with a tiny bat on it, dangling from the branch of a tree – and another map pebble.

"I still say it's dodgy," he said.

"Yeah ... but Lily's a black belt in karate," said Alina.

Ben shrugged and jumped down. "OK then," he said. "Let's go."

5 Stone-cold truth

They were nearly at the pathway to the valley when they heard a puffing sound. Turning around they saw Lily's dad running after them.

"Your mum sent me," he wheezed. "She got worried you might all get stolen."

Lily rolled her eyes. "*Dad!* I'm a BLACK BELT in karate."

"Also," grinned Mr Dillow, "I want to know the answer to the great Pebble Puzzle!"

They all climbed down the steep, rough steps, through the trees, and along a path to the wooden bridge over the stream – where they stopped and stared. Both wooden handrails were *covered* in painted pebbles – each with a few words on.

"Go on," said Ben. "Read it!"

Dev walked alongside the pebble sentence, reading
out loud:

"Thank you for coming. This valley needs you.
The stream is full of rubbish. The paths are covered in
takeaway boxes and plastic cups. These things are …"

Dev turned and walked back, reading along
the other rail.

"… choking nature. Only you can save this valley and
all the creatures who live in it. You know what to do."

"Look!" yelled Alina, pointing. Tied to a tree was a big
sack, filled with rubber gloves and carrier bags.

Slowly, they turned around, scanning the trees.
Was the Pebble Painter here now?

Dev looked at the stream. It was clogged with three
old tyres, a rusty bike and loads of empty drink cans.
The path was strewn with cartons, wipes and bottles.
He felt ashamed. He remembered letting that ice
lolly wrapper just fly away into the trees yesterday
without bothering to chase it. He hadn't picked up
the milkshake carton in the grass either.

"Seriously?" said Ben. "All of this ... just so we can pick up litter?"

Alina stared at him. "*Look* at this place!" she said. "It's terrible! Why didn't we notice this before? It's *our* valley. We have to save it."

"Yes," said Dev. "Starting now. Because ... we've all dropped this stuff, haven't we?

"Seriously? *I'm* not spending my weekend picking up rubbish," muttered Ben. "You can if you want to."

Everyone watched in silence as he turned around and stomped back up the steep path.

"Stupid pebbles," he muttered. He'd thought they were going to have a proper adventure and now he was on his own because Dev wanted to drag mucky tyres out of a stream all day.

Ben pulled the three pebbles out of his pocket and threw them into the undergrowth. They rattled against a plastic bottle and some crunched up fast food wrappers. Ben stopped and stared at the rubbish. Then he looked along the edge of the path and saw crisp packets caught in the brambles and an old broken scooter upside down in a bush.

Ben half turned back. Maybe ... maybe he *should* help. Then he turned away again. Oh, come *on*.

A pebble rolled out across the path in front of him. This one had a bee on it. It said "HELP!" on the back.

"I'm not DOING it!" he yelled into the trees. "It's not MY job!"

The trees just rustled back.

He stomped on towards home for another minute before the *next* pebble arrived. This one had a hedgehog on it.

HELP!

"Aaaaargh!" Ben turned around and marched back to the valley.

6 Rock on

"This is the best day *ever*," said Dev. There was mud on his face and his hair was stuck up.

The bit of valley by the bridge and the stream looked as beautiful as a painting.

His mum and dad were sorting through the bin bags for stuff that could be recycled. As soon as they had arrived, they'd wanted to help. Then Mr Dillow had nipped home for a wheelbarrow to collect the old tyres and rusty bike to take to the council tip.

"We're going to come down here and keep it lovely," said Alina. "Every week."

"Even *Ben*?" asked her mum, grinning.

Ben stood up and waved his hands in their plastic gloves. "Even BEN!" he said, grinning. He was unexpectedly proud of what they'd done.

On the way home, Dev said: "Just one thing ... who IS the Pebble Painter?"

There was a ping. A perfectly round pebble rolled across the path. On it was a blue dragonfly with filmy wings. On the other side was ...

'Thank you'.

They looked up and around ... but the Pebble Painter was nowhere to be seen.

THE PUGGLE

PEBBLE PUZZLE LEADS TO VALLEY CLEAR UP

THE PEOPLE OF PUGGLE have cleaned up their local valley and river after being asked to – by PEBBLES!

Pebbles have been mysteriously arriving all over the village with paintings of wildlife on one side and the word "HELP!" on the other.

"We started getting these pebbles out of nowhere," said eight-year-old Dev Bakar. "We thought it was a joke, but yesterday the pebbles gave us a time and a place – and it was the river.

BUGLE

"A load more pebbles on the bridge asked us to do a clear up."

And not before time. Most of the villagers have now confessed that they were ashamed of how much litter had been dropped.

A group called PUGGLE PEBBLES CLEANER UPPERS has now been formed and will keep the woods and streams clean and beautiful and wildlife friendly.

But the mystery remains ... Who IS the Puggle Pebble Painter?

Ideas for reading

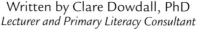

Written by Clare Dowdall, PhD
Lecturer and Primary Literacy Consultant

Reading objectives:
- discuss the sequence of events in books and how items of information are related
- make inferences on the basis of what is being said and done
- predict what might happen on the basis of what has been read so far
- draw on what they already know or on background information and vocabulary provided by the teacher

Spoken language objectives:
- articulate and justify answers, arguments and opinions
- participate in discussions, presentations, performances and debates

Curriculum links: Science – living things and their habitats; PSHE – being safe

Word count: 2488

Interest words: mind readers, magnifying glass, serpent, stone-cold truth

Resources: whiteboards, materials for conducting a clean-up campaign, paper and pencils or ICT to design posters

Build a context for reading
- Ask children to suggest what has happened to the boy on the front cover of the story, and how he might be feeling.
- Read the title and blurb together and ask children to think about what the mysterious pebbles might mean and who might be sending them.

Understand and apply reading strategies
- Read Chapter 1 with the group. Ask the children what they would do if they found the three pebbles with the word "HELP!" written on them.